Nancy Johnson

Snow-White and the Seven Dwarfs

OS VERITATIS

Snow-White and the Seven Dwarfs

A TALE FROM THE BROTHERS GRIMM TRANSLATED BY
RANDALL JARRELL · PICTURES BY NANCY EKHOLM BURKERT
FARRAR, STRAUS AND GIROUX · NEW YORK

Pictures copyright © 1972 by Nancy Ekholm Burkert
All rights reserved
Library of Congress catalog card number: 72-81489
ISBN 0-374-37099-0
Published simultaneously in Canada by Doubleday Canada Ltd., Toronto
Printed in the United States of America by Pearl Pressman Liberty
Bound by A. Horowitz and Son
Typography by Atha Tehon
Third printing, 1973

For CLAIRE

Together we are walking in the Forest
while the rhythms of light and shadow play.

N. E. B.

Once it was the middle of winter, and the snowflakes fell from the sky like feathers. At a window with a frame of ebony a queen sat and sewed. And as she sewed and looked out at the snow, she pricked her finger with the needle, and three drops of blood fell in the snow. And in the white snow the red looked so beautiful that she thought to herself: "If only I had a child as white as snow, as red as blood, and as black as the wood in the window frame!"

And after a while she had a little daughter as white as snow, as red as blood, and with hair as black as ebony, and because of that she was called Snow-White. And when the child was born, the queen died.

After a year the king took himself another wife. She was a beautiful woman, but she was proud and haughty and could not bear that anyone should be more beautiful than she. She had a wonderful mirror, and when she stood in front of it and looked in it and said:

> *Mirror, mirror on the wall,*
> *Who is fairest of us all?*

then the mirror would answer:

> *Queen, thou art the fairest of us all!*

Then she was satisfied, because she knew that the mirror spoke the truth.

But Snow-White kept growing, and kept growing more beautiful, and when she was seven years old, she was as beautiful as the bright day, and more beautiful than the Queen herself. Once when she asked her mirror:

> *Mirror, mirror on the wall,*
> *Who is fairest of us all?*

it answered:

Queen, thou art the fairest in this hall,
But Snow-White's fairer than us all.

Then the Queen was horrified, and grew yellow and green with envy. From that hour on, whenever she saw Snow-White the heart in her body would turn over, she hated the girl so. And envy and pride, like weeds, kept growing higher and higher in her heart, so that day and night she had no peace. Then she called a huntsman and said: "Take the child out into the forest, I don't want to lay eyes on her again. You kill her, and bring me her lung and liver as a token."

The hunter obeyed, and took her out, and when he had drawn his hunting knife and was about to pierce Snow-White's innocent heart, she began to weep and said: "Oh, dear huntsman, spare my life! I'll run off into the wild forest and never come home again." And because she was so beautiful, the huntsman pitied her and said: "Run away then, you poor child."

"Soon the wild beasts will have eaten you," he thought, and yet it was as if a stone had been lifted from his heart not to have to kill her. And as a young boar just then came running by, he killed it, cut out its lung and liver, and brought them to the Queen as a token. The cook had to cook them in salt, and the wicked woman ate them up and thought that she had eaten Snow-White's lung and liver.

Now the poor child was all, all alone in the great forest, and so terrified that she stared at all the leaves on the trees and didn't know what to do. She began to run, and ran over the sharp stones and through the thorns, and the wild beasts sprang past her, but they did her no harm.

She ran on till her feet wouldn't go any farther, and when it was almost evening she saw a little house and went inside to rest. Inside the house everything was small, but cleaner and neater than words will say. In the middle there stood a little table with a white tablecloth, and on it were seven little plates, each plate with its own spoon, and besides that, seven little knives and forks and seven little mugs. Against the wall were seven little beds, all in a row, spread with snow-white sheets. Because she was so hungry and thirsty, Snow-White ate a little of the vegetables and bread from each of the little plates, and drank a drop of wine from each little mug, since she didn't want to take all of anybody's. After that, because she was so tired, she lay down in a bed, but not a one would fit; this one was too long, the other was too short, and so on, until finally the seventh was just right, and she lay down in it, said her prayers, and went to sleep.

As soon as it had got all dark, the owners of the house came back. These were seven dwarfs who dug and delved for ore in the mountains. They lighted their seven little candles, and as soon as it got light in their little house, they saw that someone had been inside, because everything wasn't the way they'd left it.

The first said: "Who's been sitting in my little chair?"
The second said: "Who's been eating out of my little plate?"
The third said: "Who's been taking some of my bread?"
The fourth said: "Who's been eating my vegetables?"
The fifth said: "Who's been using my little fork?"
The sixth said: "Who's been cutting with my little knife?"
The seventh said: "Who's been drinking out of my little mug?"

Then the first looked around and saw that his bed was a little mussed, so he said: "Who's been lying on my little bed?" The others came running and cried out: "Someone's been lying in mine too." But the seventh, when he looked in his bed, saw Snow-White, who was lying in it fast asleep.

He called the others, who came running up and shouted in astonishment, holding up their little candles so that the light shone on Snow-White. "Oh my goodness gracious! Oh my goodness gracious!" cried they, "how beautiful the child is!" And they were so happy that they didn't wake her, but let her go on sleeping in the little bed. The seventh dwarf, though, slept with the others, an hour with each, till the night was over.

When it was morning Snow-White awoke, and when she saw the seven dwarfs she was frightened. They were friendly, though, and asked: "What's your name?"

"I'm named Snow-White," she answered.

"How did you get to our house?" went on the dwarfs. Then she told them that her stepmother had tried to have her killed, but that the huntsman had spared her life, and that she'd run the whole day and at last had found their house.

The dwarfs said: "If you'll look after our house for us, cook, make the beds, wash, sew, and knit, and if you'll keep everything clean and neat, then you can stay with us, and you shall lack for nothing."

"Yes," said Snow-White, "with all my heart," and stayed with them. She kept their house in order: in the morning the dwarfs went to the mountains and looked for gold and ores, in the evening they came back, and then their food had to be ready for them.

In the daytime the little girl was alone, so the good dwarfs warned her and said: "Watch out for your stepmother. Soon she'll know you're here; be sure not to let anybody inside."

But the Queen, since she thought she had eaten Snow-White's lung and liver, was sure that she was the fairest of all. But one day she stood before her mirror and said:

> *Mirror, mirror on the wall,*
> *Who is fairest of us all?*

Then the mirror answered:

> *Queen, thou art the fairest that I see,*
> *But over the hills, where the seven dwarfs dwell,*
> *Snow-White is still alive and well,*
> *And there is none so fair as she.*

This horrified her, because she knew that the mirror never told a lie; and she saw that the hunter had betrayed her, and that Snow-White was still alive. And she thought and thought about how to kill her, for as long as she wasn't the fairest in all the land, her envy gave her no rest. And when at last she thought of something, she painted her face and dressed herself like an old peddler-woman, and nobody could have recognized her. In this disguise she went over the seven mountains to the seven dwarfs' house, knocked at the door, and called: "Lovely things for sale! Lovely things for sale!"

Snow-White looked out of the window and called: "Good day, dear lady, what have you to sell?"

"Good things, lovely things," she answered, "bodice-laces of all colors," and she pulled out one that was woven of many-colored silk.

"It will be all right to let in the good old woman," thought Snow-White, unbolted the door, and bought herself some pretty laces.

"Child," said the old woman, "how it does become you! Come, I'll lace you up properly." Snow-White hadn't the least suspicion, and let the old woman lace her up with the new laces. But she laced so tight and laced so fast that it took Snow-White's breath away, and she fell down as if she were dead. "Now you're the most beautiful again," said the Queen to herself, and hurried away.

Not long after, at evening, the seven dwarfs came home, but how shocked they were to see their dear Snow-White lying on the ground; and she didn't move and she didn't stir, as if she were dead. They lifted her up, and when they saw how tightly she was laced, they cut the laces in two; then she began to breathe a little, and little by little returned to consciousness. When the dwarfs heard what had happened, they said: "The old peddler-woman was no one else but that wicked Queen; be careful, don't ever let another soul inside when we're not with you."

But the wicked Queen, as soon as she'd got home, stood in front of the mirror and asked:

> *Mirror, mirror on the wall,*
> *Who is fairest of us all?*

It answered the same as ever:

> *Queen, thou art the fairest that I see,*
> *But over the hills, where the seven dwarfs dwell,*
> *Snow-White is still alive and well,*
> *And there is none so fair as she.*

When she heard this all the blood rushed to her heart, she was so horrified, for she saw plainly that Snow-White was alive again. "But now," said she, "I'll think of something that really will put an end to you," and with the help of witchcraft, which she understood, she made a poisoned comb. Then she dressed herself up and took the shape of another old woman. So she went over the seven mountains to the seven dwarfs' house, knocked on the door, and called: "Lovely things for sale! Lovely things for sale!"

Snow-White looked out and said: "You may as well go on, I'm not allowed to let anybody in."

"But surely you're allowed to look," said the old woman, and she took out the poisoned comb and held it up. It looked so nice to the child that she let herself be fooled, and opened the door. When they'd agreed on the price the old woman said: "Now, for once, I'll comb your hair properly." Poor Snow-White didn't suspect anything, and let the old woman do as she pleased. But hardly had she put the comb in Snow-White's hair than the poison in it began to work, and the girl fell down unconscious. "You paragon of beauty," cried the wicked woman, "now you're done for," and went away.

By good luck, though, it was almost evening, when the seven dwarfs came home. When they saw Snow-White lying on the ground as if she were dead, right away they suspected the stepmother and looked and found the poisoned comb. Hardly had they drawn it out than Snow-White returned to consciousness, and told them what had happened. Then they warned her all over again to stay in the house and open the door to no one.

At home the Queen stood in front of the mirror and said:

> *Mirror, mirror on the wall,*
> *Who is fairest of us all?*

It answered the same as ever:

> *Queen, thou art the fairest that I see,*
> *But over the hills, where the seven dwarfs dwell,*
> *Snow-White is still alive and well,*
> *And there is none so fair as she.*

When she heard the mirror say that, she shook with rage. "Snow-White shall die," cried she, "even if it costs me my own life!" Then she went to a very secret, lonely room that no one ever came to, and there she made a poisoned apple. On the outside it was beautiful, white with red cheeks, so that anyone who saw it wanted it; but whoever ate even the least bite of it would die.

When the apple was ready she painted her face and disguised herself as a farmer's wife, and then went over the seven mountains to the seven dwarfs' house. She knocked, and Snow-White put her head out of the window and said: "I'm not allowed to let anybody in, the seven dwarfs told me not to."

"That's all right with me," answered the farmer's wife. "I'll get rid of my apples without any trouble. Here, I'll give you one."

"No," said Snow-White, "I'm afraid to take it."

"Are you afraid of poison?" said the old woman. "Look, I'll cut the apple in two halves; you eat the red cheek and I'll eat the white." But the apple was so cunningly made that only the red part was poisoned. Snow-White longed for the lovely apple, and when she saw that the old woman was eating it, she couldn't resist it any longer, put out her hand, and took the poisoned half. But hardly had she a bite of it in her mouth than she fell down on the ground dead. Then the Queen gave her a dreadful look, laughed aloud, and cried: "White as snow, red as blood, black as ebony! This time the dwarfs can't wake you!"

And when, at home, she asked the mirror:

> *Mirror, mirror on the wall,*
> *Who is fairest of us all?*

at last it answered:

> *Queen, thou art the fairest of us all.*

Then her envious heart had rest, as far as an envious heart can have rest.

When they came home at evening, the dwarfs found Snow-White lying on the ground. No breath came from her mouth, and she was dead. They lifted her up, looked to see if they could find anything poisonous, unlaced her, combed her hair, washed her with water and wine, but nothing helped; the dear child was dead and stayed dead.

They laid her on a bier, and all seven of them sat down and wept for her, and wept for three whole days. Then they were going to bury her, but she still looked as fresh as though she were alive, and still had her beautiful red cheeks. They said: "We can't bury her in the black ground," and had made for her a coffin all of glass, into which one could see from every side, laid her in it, and wrote her name on it in golden letters, and that she was a king's daughter. Then they set the coffin out on the mountainside, and one of them always stayed by it and guarded it. And the animals, too, came and wept over Snow-White—first an owl, then a raven, and last of all a dove.

Now Snow-White lay in the coffin for a long, long time, and her body didn't decay. She looked as if she were sleeping, for she was still as white as snow, as red as blood, and her hair was as black as ebony. But a king's son happened to come into the forest and went to the dwarfs' house to spend the night. He saw the coffin on the mountain, and the beautiful Snow-White inside, and read what was written on it in golden letters. Then he said to the dwarfs: "Let me have the coffin. I'll give you anything that you want for it."

But the dwarfs answered: "We wouldn't give it up for all the gold in the world."

Then he said: "Give it to me then, for I can't live without seeing Snow-White. I'll honor and prize her as my own beloved." When he spoke so, the good dwarfs took pity on him and gave him the coffin.

Now the king's son had his servants carry it away on their shoulders.

The servants happened to stumble over a bush, and with the shock the poisoned piece of apple that Snow-White had bitten off came out of her throat. And in a little while she opened her eyes, lifted the lid of the coffin, sat up, and was alive again. "Oh, heavens, where am I?" cried she.

The king's son, full of joy, said: "You're with me," and told her what had happened, and said: "I love you more than anything in all the world. Come with me to my father's palace; you shall be my wife." And Snow-White loved him and went with him, and her wedding was celebrated with great pomp and splendor.

But Snow-White's wicked stepmother was invited to the feast. When she had put on her beautiful clothes, she stepped in front of the mirror and said:

> *Mirror, mirror on the wall,*
> *Who is fairest of us all?*

The mirror answered:

> *Queen, thou art the fairest in this hall,*
> *But the young queen's fairer than us all.*

Then the wicked woman cursed and was so terrified and miserable, so completely miserable, that she didn't know what to do. At first she didn't want to go to the wedding at all, but it gave her no peace; she had to go and see the young queen. And as she went in she recognized Snow-White and, what with rage and terror, she stood there and couldn't move.

But they had already put iron slippers over a fire of coals, and they brought them in with tongs and set them before her. Then she had to put on the red-hot slippers and dance till she dropped down dead.

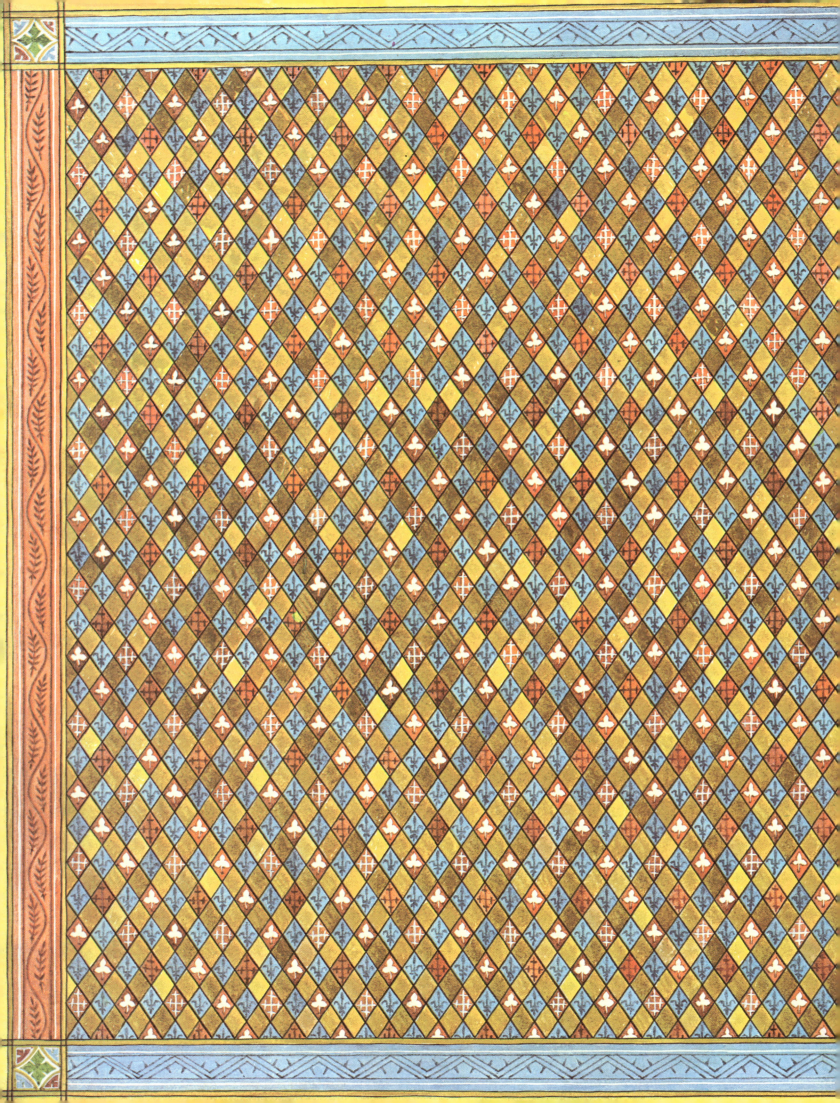